LICKETY SPLIT

WHO ARE YOU?

Written and illustrated by
Harland Williams

Penworthy
PUBLISHING COMPANY
219 NORTH MILWAUKEE ST., MILWAUKEE, WISCONSIN 53202

PRINTED IN HONG KONG

0-87617-054-8

Down by the pond on a bright summer morning,
Lickety saw his reflection and found it quite boring.

His sides were too fat, and his neck much too long.
He was sure his creator had done something wrong.

His legs were too short, his tail slowed him down,
His skin was too green, and his head far too round.

As he sat and reflected, a blur caught his eye,
A shadow passed over. It had come from the sky!

Far, far above him, a winged reptile soared,
And Lickety decided that he was quite bored!

"I'm tired of being me," young Lickety said,
As the reptile flew down, over Lickety's head.

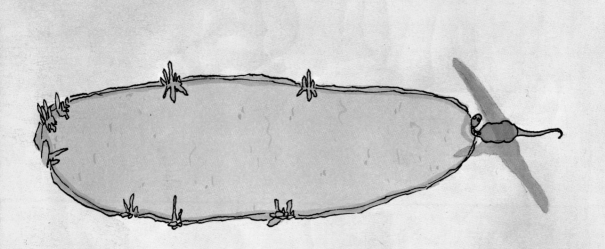

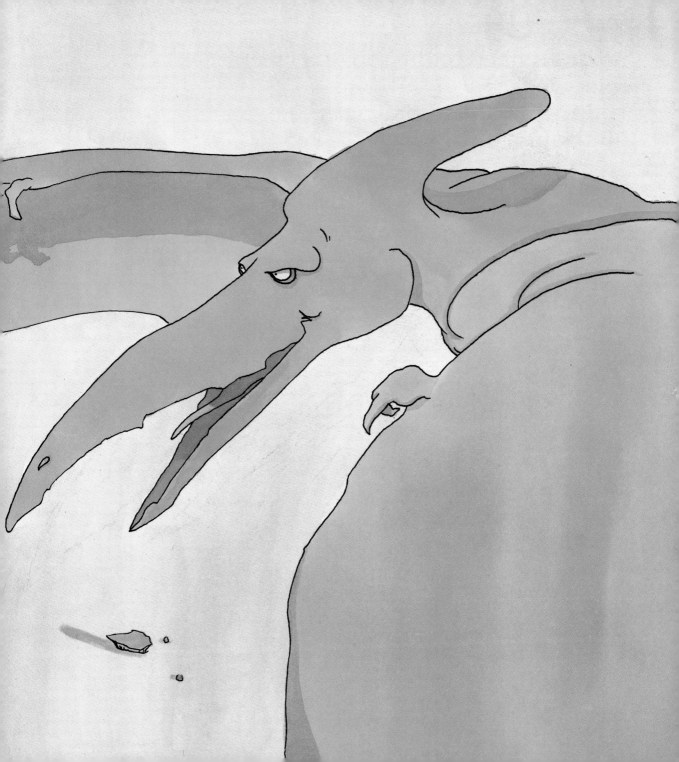

So he climbed to the top of a steep, rocky ledge.
"I'll fly like the birds!" was the dinosaur's pledge.

Lickety ran on the cliff,
till his feet left the ground.
Good grief! He was airborne!
All ten thousand pounds!

The sky was so clear.
It was great flying weather.
But it was hard to stay up.
Oh! For some feathers!

For a moment he hung there,
as proud as could be,
Till, still flapping his arms,
he plunged to the sea.

Suddenly surrounded by a wet world of wonder,
Lickety held in his breath. He was forty feet under!

"Why, this is just perfect. I've been granted my wish.
No more landlubbing for me, I will live like a fish."

Other creatures soon gathered
to watch Lickety swim.
"You might find it easier if you'd
try growing fins."

Embarrassed and sad, with his last
puff of air,
Lickety swam to the shore thinking,
"Life's just not fair."

Clearly, he could not live
in the sky or the sea.
But for sure he could live
like an ape in a tree!

"Ha, ha," Lickety hollered.
"I've found it at last.
Now my dinosaur days
are a thing of the past!"

So he started his new life,
just a branch at a time.
He went right to the top
before ending his climb.

"What an achievement,"
thought Lickety.
" The new me has been found.
Why these apes have it made!
You can see all around!"

The tree started swaying with Lickety's
ten thousand pounds.
Then that very tall tree bent right down
to the ground.

Lickety had a great thought as he
lay in the dirt.
"Why, I'll try underground where
I CAN'T be hurt!"

Lickety tightened his claws and
dug up the ground.
He was sure his identity now
would be found.

He tunneled and shoveled, till everything
was dark,
And was shocked when a gopher
exclaimed with a bark:

"Get out of my home. You're too big
for this place!"
But his bark softened slightly
when he saw the sad face.

"I'm sorry I shouted, but what I tell
you is true.
Eating lugworms and beetle bugs
just isn't for you."

So Lickety slowly climbed out, he'd
reached the end of his rope.
But then a creature flashed by
and filled him with hope.

A bouncy beast with long, thin legs,
whose obvious gift was speed.
"That's it! Of course! To change myself,
fast movement is what I need!"

So with a smile spread wide on his dinosaur face, Lickety switched to high gear and took up the race!

He found it quite easy to match the
strange creature's pace,
Then the creature stopped playing,
and ZOOMED into space!

Looking after the creature,
his heart about to burst,
Lickety stopped on the road
and cried in the dirt.

His long search was over.
He'd tried at every cost,
To be someone special,
but his quest was now lost.

Alone in the grass, Lickety felt
he had failed,
Then the silence broke and a
distant lizard wailed.

He stretched up his neck to see
the cause of such commotion.
When he realized what it was,
he went into motion.

A giant swooping bird snatched a child
from its mother.
It was now, Lickety realized, he had
the ability of no other.

He ran his hardest and stretched his neck
as far as it would go.
He snatched the baby from the bird
(luckily, he caught its toe!).

The mother lizard was overjoyed with such
a courageous deed.
"Oh, thank you, Lickety! You came in my
time of need."

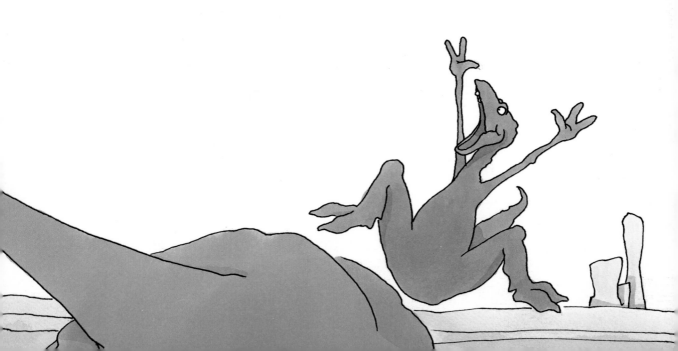

"You've saved my child's life, young fella,
and rescued him from danger.
You really are quite special for helping
a total stranger."

"No one else has a big, long neck that
can stretch so very high.
I'm very glad you are who you are."
And then she bid him goodbye.

Lickety felt wonderful. What the mother
had said was true.
Then he looked inside himself and thought,
"I'm glad I'm me, too."

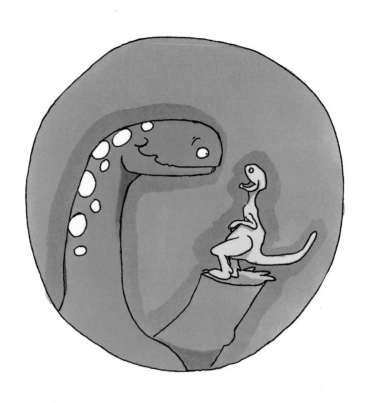